A Diary of
Snap Wolf's Journey to Find a Mate

A Diary of Snap Wolf's Journey to Find a Mate

A coming of age story about a wolf's struggle to become an alpha

MORRIS R. PIKE

with illustrations by Chris Sheets

One's Company
PO Box 5606
Salem, Oregon 97304

 Published 2016 in paperback.
Also available in Kindle format — first published in 2015.
Printed in the United States of America

ISBN: 978-0-692-75912-7
Library of Congress Control Number: 2016912028

To my great grandsons Myles, Koen, and Wesley Harris
and to
OR7, the wolf on whose real-life journey this story is based

WASHINGTON
Portland
OREGON
Eugene
IDAHO
NEVADA
CALIFORNIA
N
W
E
S

Contents

Preface

Fascinated by the real-life story of a brave young wolf going to incredible lengths to find a mate and become a leader of his own pack, I wanted to create a story about what it might have been like along the way. It is a story about setting goals and never giving up. My love of nature gave me the excuse to follow OR7's 1200-mile route and my imagination added the rest.

For those who may struggle with some of the big or strange words, I have provided definitions in the back of this book. The places in Oregon that are listed in the story are real and may be searched on the Internet. There are many good topics for discussion in this story of perseverance, kindness and compassion.

Thanks to the many people who helped me write about Snap. Nature specialists Larry Rea and Marvin Kellar kept me straightened out about nature and wildlife and without the wisdom of farmer/rancher Mac Stewart I would not have understood that animals just do what animals do.

I'm indebted to Jan Jackson who wore herself out keeping me from smelling every flower along the way . . .

She kept me focused on story. This book is her book too. I thank my editor Eileen DiCicco, the Oregon Fish and Wildlife who placed the electronic collar on OR7 so we could follow his journey and my many friends and colleagues who were kind enough to read and re-read my story.

—Morris R. Pike

~ 1 ~

The move to Oregon

Snap Wolf lifted his nose and sniffed air. The blue haze that filled Hells Canyon nearly obscured the pale string of the *Snake River* that flowed below him on the valley floor.

Squinting his eyes to defeat the glare of the low-hanging sun, he scanned the distant mountains to the west.

Alpha, his father, was about to lead his pack across the river and settle them in the *Wallowa Mountains* of Oregon. Snap had always wondered what lay on the other side of the river and now he was going to find out. The Idaho wolves were meeting with them to say goodbye.

Meanwhile, across the river, patches of pine trees and other hardy vegetation struggled to sustain themselves. However the clusters of trees and bushes didn't complain . . . they seemed to understand that their job was to provide food and shelter for the birds and animals that lived there.

For centuries, the animals and birds that made the Wallowa Mountains their home, took advantage of the provisions the forests and prairie grasses provided. The animals and birds didn't tell them that they loved them . . . but the trees and grasses knew.

~~~

Meanwhile, the porcupines were petrified when they heard the wolves from Idaho were returning to the Wallowa's. The badgers spread the word that soon everyone would be seeing gray wolves.

These *Horse Creek* dwellers, which were sure that the news would panic everyone, were surprised when they all simply shrugged and went about living their lives. The other birds and animals knew that all they could do about it was to stay alert. They understood that no matter what, the wolves were going do what wolves do and they knew that they would continue to do what they did.

As for the humans who lived there, they were a mystery to all the animals. Yes, humans also do what
~~~

humans do, but the animals never knew exactly what that was going to be.

~~~

Alpha brought his pack into Wallowa territory and settled in the *Imnaha Valley*. He sniffed every rock, tree and bush searching for evidence of other wolf packs. He led a series of threatening howls to warn any wolves within earshot to leave or at least stay clear. So far no one had dared to challenge his leadership and it didn't look like anyone would do so very soon.

He ordered his pack members to explore the wooded hills and pastureland along the *Imnaha River* to make sure there was a good food supply. They found the area well populated with both large and small animals. Alpha was confident that he and his powerful family would own the Oregon Wallowa territory.
~~~

~ 2 ~

Leaving the pack

Snap took a deep breath of clear mountain air. He felt strong. His muscles rippled complementing the handsome frame of the powerful wolf he'd grown to be.

But the question of what it would be like to be an alpha wolf gnawed at him.

'There can be only one alpha wolf in the pack,' he thought. 'I need to challenge my father for leadership or leave and establish my own pack. It is a decision every male wolf must make . . . a decision I must make . . . it's the way of wolves. To stay would be to remain subservient

. . . like my brothers who follow the old one like helpless sheep.'

But if he left, he knew he would lose the security of the pack. He would face the hidden dangers in the formidable *Blue Mountains.*

He stood for a long while contemplating the possible move. Dare he leave the *Imnaha* pack and search for a mate?

It was spring . . . the time for Alpha and his prime female to produce new pups to enlarge the pack.

'I can't stay,' Snap thought. "I must leave, find a mate and become an alpha male of my own pack."

He looked closely at the healthy, white petals of a woodland strawberry. "You get to be a beautiful, five-petaled white flower with yellow whiskers in the center of your face as long as you live . . . Is that fun?"

Of course, the strawberry didn't respond. It just beamed in the rays of the bright sun.

In bending down he inadvertently kicked a cluster of dandelion seeds sending them sailing into the gentle breeze.

"And you get to go wherever the wind takes you," he said watching the tiny parachutes floating . . . growing smaller and smaller against the azure sky.

Night was coming on. Snap rose on his haunches, sniffed the air, and trotted over the straw-colored grass to join his lounging pack. He spent the remaining twilight moments walking among them looking at each of his beautiful sisters and strong handsome brothers.

He stopped to admire his mother. He'd find a mate like her. He looked at his father. 'He is a good alpha male,' Snap thought, ' . . . a good example for me.'

He lay down with his chin between his outstretched paws, closed his eyes and went to sleep.

~ 3 ~

The journey begins

The faint glow of morning appeared over the jagged crest of the mountains east of *Cayuse Meadow*. Snap lifted himself to a standing position and surveyed his sleeping family. He was starting a journey . . . a journey to fulfill an ancient urge that gnaws at all male wolves.

Throughout the day, he followed faint animal trails paralleling the Imnaha River. He wasn't in a hurry, but he did want to be far enough away that there was little likelihood that Alpha or any of his brothers would come after him.

He was glad that the bird's singing was the only sound that broke the silence in the forest. He liked birds . . . their songs were company.

Circling vultures told him that carrion was near. A deer may have fallen off a bluff and died. He trotted toward them. After eating his fill, he found a patch of lupine, finessed it into a suitable bed and lay down.

Suddenly, he heard a rustling nearby. Nerves alerted and muscles tensed, Snap was ready to defend himself. He was surprised to see a red fox creeping into his space.

The fox looked up at him and froze. She had never seen anything like him before.

"What are you? I've never se, se, seen . . . "

"A wolf . . . I'm a wolf," Snap reassured. "Snap's my name . . . What's yours?"

"Amber. Where did you come from, Sn, Sn . . . Snap? What are you doing here?"

"Looking for a wolf mate . . . You seen any wolves around here?"

"Never seen one before . . . " Amber answered timidly, letting her guard down a bit. "You're big," she managed to add.

Snap laughed, "You're small . . . You alone?"

"No, there are a lot of us hanging out in these buttes. You wouldn't hurt us foxes, would you?"

"Not unless you give me cause," Snap answered.

"Then, you can stay here with us, if you like. The others will love it . . . I'll bet you can whip a cougar."

"Whip a cougar? Done it before," Snap answered confidently.

"I gotta get back to the rest . . . Gotta tell them . . . " Amber said.

Snap watched her go. "Pretty fox."

As the setting sun glowed in the west, Snap gazed at the silhouette of the black mountains. He had done it. He'd left the security of his powerful father's pack. A shudder gripped his body. He was alone now. As cute as the fox was . . . foxes would not do. He had to search until he could find a mate. He had to become the alpha of his own pack.

In the distance Snap could hear a mournful howl. It was his mother's voice calling for him.

He stirred, tempted to run to her. He trotted a hundred yards or so in the direction of the beckoning call.

He stopped. 'No!' He'd answered an ancient urge . . . it compelled him to set his feet into the unknown. He did not answer the howl but returned to his bed and settled down.

Before falling asleep he mused, 'Tomorrow, I'll sniff the free mountain air and strike out . . . follow *Beeler Ridge* . . . south.'

~ 4 ~

Dangerous heights

The early morning sun pried Snap from sleep. He stretched his legs, yawned and trotted to the remnants of the fallen deer. After satisfying his hunger, he drank water from a pocket honed in a large rock and galloped west over the bare ground of the mountain ridge.

Creeks and rivers were refreshing and necessary, but Snap preferred to travel the crests of buttes. Standing on the edge of a bluff with an unobstructed view in all directions made him feel . . . almost . . . like an alpha.

'And I will be, when I find a mate,' he thought prancing like the thoroughbred Appaloosa he'd seen dancing in the meadows of the *Salmon River* in Idaho.

Then, almost unknowingly, he found himself carefully inching his way along a jagged ledge etched into the southern face of the mountain. On his right were granite walls reaching into the sky above him, and on his left below were tons of loose rock. One slip and he would tumble hundreds of feet down the treacherous surface.

He wished he'd chosen a different route, but never having traveled this way before, he didn't know. Trampled tufts of grass and well-placed rocks were evidence that other animals also used the ledge to negotiate the dangerous terrain.

He heard a click. He looked toward the sound not knowing what to expect. There above him was a mountain goat. It had sharp horns . . . no doubt to use as a weapon when needed.

It appeared to Snap that the goat was in a precarious position also. One of its hind hoofs was gripping a buried rock and the other stretched toward a narrow indentation in the stone wall. The skilled mountain climber was attempting to move from one dangerous situation to another.

Ordinarily, Snap had no reason to fear a goat. He had seen mountain goats in Idaho. His pack had brought down more than one. On flat ground goats are no-match for wolves. But in the mountains . . .

This goat wasn't afraid of Snap either. In his element on rocky mountainsides no predator can touch a skilled mountain climber like himself. In the lowlands, bobcats, lions, coyotes, and bears prey on mountain goats, but not in the alpine.

But, he had never seen an animal like this one, and didn't know what to think.

"Are you a coyote . . . a big one?" the goat asked, lifting himself onto the ridge above Snap. "I guess not," he said looking down. " . . . they have narrow faces . . . yours is broad . . . strong."

"I'm not a coyote," Snap said, a bit uneasy. He knew that it wouldn't take much for the goat to catch him with a horn and send him hurtling to his death on the rocks below.

If the goat made that choice, Snap would defend himself the best he could . . . he'd take the goat with him if it came to a fight. He waited for the goat to respond. After a few moments it was apparent that he and the goat were at an impasse.

"I'm a wolf," Snap said breaking the silence. "I came from the mountains east of here."

"The *Seven Devils* . . . huh?" the goat said lifting his massive head and gazing at the mountain peaks to the east . . . "Snow this time of year means they're high . . . that's good for us goats . . . bears and . . . you know, can't get to us. But I've never been there."

"Why?" Snap asked taking a careful step along the ledge toward a large boulder clinging to the cliff's southern face.

"Don't know," the goat answered, "We're here in the Wallowa's . . . that's all I know . . . we've always been here . . . gets easier on the other side," the goat said moving above and out of sight."

Snap looked up. There was no sign of the goat. "I have to go back," Snap called. He backed up to a place where he thought he might turn around.

The goat re-appeared. "Climb up here. It'll be easy going for you." He paused and surveyed the plateau on which he stood and added, " . . . at least for a while."

Snap looked down. A fall to the rocks below would be fatal. He couldn't go back the way he came. "If I come up . . . you won't butt me off the cliff . . . will you?"

"I won't if you promise not to eat me," the goat answered.

"Eat you?" Snap asked perplexed. In his predicament, eating was the last thing on his mind.

Then, he realized that the goat's own sense of self-preservation was what made him cautious. And he recognized that the goat was right to be fearful . . . eating cloven hooved creatures is what wolves do when they are hungry.

Though the goat had never seen a wolf, he was wise to be cautious.

"Eat you . . . I won't!" Snap reassured and began making his way up the steep grade and onto the flat surface on top.

The goat backed away, uncertain the wolf would keep his word.

"Don't worry, we don't need to fight," Snap said taking an easy step toward him. "We can be friends, can't we? My name is Snap, what's yours?"

The goat seemed to relax . . . but kept a reasonable distance between himself and the wolf. He wagged his head up and down. His long goatee moved to its rhythm.

"Ted . . . Ted Goat's my name.

"Snap. I've never seen anything like you. What are you doing here where you don't belong?"

"I had to leave my pack in the Imnaha . . . Cayuse Meadow to be exact," Snap answered.

"Had to?"

"I don't understand why I had to, but I had to . . . my dad, the alpha wolf, won't allow any rival to take his place at the head of the pack . . . so I had to leave or be subservient," he complained. "Doesn't seem fair . . . does it? Did you say there are no wolves in these mountains?"

"Not that I've seen . . . but there will be if you stay," Ted said grinning. "You can become a part of my tribe, if you like. This is a wonderful place to live . . . lots to eat . . . "

Nibbling a sprig of sage he added, "there are three high peaks to roam on." He pointed south. "A little way beyond *Granite Mountain* over there is *Pine Lake*. It's the best. You'd like it here."

"Yeah . . . maybe . . . but not for long. There's this nagging urge," Snap said thoughtfully.

"You can stay the night . . . can you not?"

"Yeah, I can do that . . . but let's get off this rock . . . Ten thousand feet in the air is above my comfort level."

The new acquaintances carefully made their way down the south face of *Red Mountain* to a grove of bull pine and settled down for the night. Snap fell asleep thinking, 'Tomorrow, I'll find wolves . . . for sure.'

~ 5 ~

Helping the pika

Snap spent the next several days hiking the elk and deer trails that transverse the Blue Mountains of *Wallowa County.*

Every night before falling asleep he squatted before his chosen resting place, stuck his nose in the air, and emitted a mournful howl. Ordinarily, a wolf traveling alone avoids howling for fear he will alert an alien pack of wolves and invite attack. But Snap was too lonely.

After each howl he sat motionless, straining his

sensitive ears in hopes of being rewarded by an answering wolf howl. So far his attempts were met with silence.

~~~

Snap hadn't traveled two miles in the new direction when he encountered an American pika harvesting hay among the large chunks of basalt that covered the mountainside.

The fuzzy creature didn't notice him. Snap quietly settled on his haunches and observed.

"Dum de dum . . . de-diddle de dum," the wooly animal sang as she scurried, carrying tufts of yellow straw in and out of a hole near a large boulder.

Snap admired her energy and the intimate little song she sang.

'A lot of work with little results,' he thought. 'I could scout up five years worth of fodder in a fraction of the time it takes that little thing to gather one.'

When the pika disappeared with a mouth full of hay, Snap stirred up a bundle and scooted it toward the cave entrance and settled behind a large rock to see what she would do when she discovered the gift.

The pika scurried out of the hole past Snap's haystack toward the harvest field. Suddenly, she stopped.

She looked back at the bonanza of straw, and then around to see what had brought it . . . she only saw rocks and meager stands of bluebunch wheatgrass, a few hardy flowers, and sagebrush struggling to hold onto life.
~~~

Scurrying back to the pile of straw, she gathered a mouth full, and disappeared into her underground silo.

Snap pushed another collection of dried grass near the entrance and again hid behind the rock. Shortly, the pika reappeared. This time she stopped at the pile of straw and sniffed it. Frightened, she quickly ran back into the opening and disappeared.

Within seconds her face appeared . . . looking to see what was doing her work.

"A funny way to spend your days," Snap said stepping out from behind the rock.

The pika disappeared again.

"I was just trying to help you do whatever it is you are doing."

"Help . . . what's that?" the tiny voice asked.

"Gather weeds to put in the hole."

"Food for the cold time," the pika said. "Who are you?"

"Snap Wolf . . . I'm just passing through."

"Never seen anything like you before. What are you doing here?"

"Never seen a wolf, huh? That's not a good sign. I'm looking for wolves."

"Well, you won't see any around here," the pika snapped and then, in softer tones added, "as far as I know."

"I won't keep you from your food harvest, I'll be on my way."

"Which way you going?"

Snap nodded south. "That way."

"Can I hitch a ride? There's a pack of pika living down in the canyon . . . takes me forever to get there . . . short legs," the pika said.

"Sure! Hop on. What's your name?"

"Roxanne," the pika said scurrying onto a rock and then onto Snap's back.

"Hold on, Roxanne. I like to trot. We'll be there in no time."

Roxanne gripped the hair on the back of Snap's neck with her mouth and held on.

Snap trotted downhill, careful to avoid jarring moves. "Eat straw all winter?" he asked.

"Ummmeeguf neu mmmnner," Roxanne mumbled through her teeth to avoid letting go of Snap's fur.

"I get it," Snap said, and entering the shade of a stand of pole trees added, "You'll never guess what wolves eat."

"NNNummm . . . Mmmmmennneauf," Roxanne muffled, maintaining her grip.

Snap laughed, sensing that Roxanne might have figured it out. "You don't need to worry . . . I'll not eat you . . . prefer bigger stuff. And besides, you're cute."

"Oooumner," Roxanne managed.

Though Roxanne couldn't talk, Snap was glad she hitched a ride. Small companionship was better than no companionship at all. They dropped down a couple thousand feet into a stand of spruce.

"Ummmmm nnnner," Roxanne mumbled.

Snap stopped. "I didn't get that. Actually, didn't get anything you've said."

"This is where I get off," Roxanne said, hopping off Snap's back onto a bed of needles.

"You sure? Didn't mean to scare you . . . you're safe with me," the young wolf reassured.

"I'm glad for that . . . you did give me a start. But no . . . I'm getting off because we're here . . . hay-stacker relatives. Thanks for the ride!" she said and scampered off into the green understory.

Snap watched Roxanne Pika go.

~ 6 ~

Taking up with Chester

The spring flowers coated the meadow and hillside with an avalanche of colors. Foxgloves were Snap's favorite, followed by beautiful Clarkia, which were bright, deep purple and looked to him something like moose antlers. He liked the looks of grassy death camas too, but had been taught by his mother to avoid tasting the inviting flower.

Remembering, Snap chuckled to himself. 'Wolves don't eat plants, mom, you know that.'

"You get hungry enough, you might eat anything," mom had said.

"Berries maybe," Snap said, " . . . but not flowers."

Traveling *Little Eagle Creek* he didn't have to worry about having to eat berries or dig up worms or munch on death camas. When he felt hungry, he was able to feed on the abundance of small animals the creek meadows nurtured.

He spotted a field of flowers growing on the hill to his right. It was a field of white mule's ears.

'Looks like snow,' Snap thought.

But when he walked into it, his large paws sank to the rocky ground below instead of riding on top like they would have in snow.

"You want to play?" Snap asked the mule's ears. He swatted a cluster with his left paw. Of course, they didn't say anything.

He was dozing, when a floppy eared rabbit hopped up.

The rabbit stared for a brief second, then, shot his strong hind legs into the ground scampering . . . his long ears flapping.

Hugging the ground, he disappeared into a nearby patch of woodland strawberries growing under a cluster of sagebrush.

"Do you live around here?" Snap asked, believing the rabbit could hear him. He stood up. He waited . . . no answer. "Do you know where the stream leads . . . where the worn paths in the tall grasses go?" He took a step toward the strawberry patch.

"I might," came a small voice from the thicket. "Who wants to know? Don't come any closer! If you do, I'll run."

"Snap Wolf wants to know."

"Never seen anything like you before . . . only dogs and coyotes . . . killer dogs and killer coyotes . . . you a coyote, a dog, or what?"

"I'm a wolf . . . like I said . . . Snap Wolf's my name . . . you can come out. I won't hurt you."

"Who said I'm afraid?"

Snap laughed.

"How do you know I won't hurt YOU?" the rabbit continued with pathetic bravado.

"Sure," Snap said warmly. "I won't harm you . . . you're pretty puny and I need your help."

"You lost or something?

"Yah . . . lost . . . in a way . . . I'm looking for other wolves like me."

Favoring his right leg, the rabbit limped from his hiding place. He stopped, squatting near the trunk of a ponderosa pine for a quick get-away if the wolf became hostile.

"What's your name?" Snap asked, surveying the gangly creature.

"Chester Rabbit," came the tentative reply.

"Chesta," Snap said smiling . . . clipping the name with his teeth. "How come you limp, Chesta?"

Chester groaned. "I'd like to say a horse stepped on me, but that would be a lie. A big rock from up hill came loose . . . came rolling down and crushed it . . . Stupid! I'm fast . . . but didn't get out of the way that time."

"Sorry about that . . . not good," Snap commiserated, looking more closely at the injured left leg.

"Well, Chesta, how about it? Have you seen any wolves around here?"

"You're the first," Chester said, monitoring the big creature's eyes.

Snap squatted on his haunches and looked at the trickle of water dancing its way south. "Do you know what it's like down there," he asked looking down stream.

"Lots of grass . . . trees . . . well, not so many as here," Chester said.

"No trees? Like the *Zumwalt Prairie*," Snap responded with concern.

"You can't eat trees. Down here there's plenty of grass."

"Grass! Great!," Snap said sarcastically.

"There's a river, too . . . Bigs call it *Powder River*. I don't know why . . . it's just water as far as I can see."

"River huh?" Snap said stepping into the shallow water of *Goose Creek* and striding down stream.

Chester, favoring his left rear leg, hopped along beside him.

"Where are you headed?" Chester asked.

"I don't know," Snap answered, "I had to leave Imnaha . . . I'm following an urge . . . an urge to be an alpha wolf . . . an urge to find a mate."

"I like it here," Chester said, hopping quickly to keep up. "I'll bet a wild carrot you would like it too . . . It's the best place . . . we're close to groves of trees . . . Look at them!" Chester demanded, stopping under the low hanging branches of a large cottonwood tree.

Snap stopped too.

"Look at them," Chester repeated. "They spread their branches out above the forest floor . . . shade and shelter for those like me who scamper for their lives. The only thing is . . . coyotes and cougars like it too . . . worse for me, but it is the way of our world."

"The way of our world," Snap repeated, mulling the phrase.

Morning light roused the two sleepers. Chester didn't want to get too far away from Snap, but he was hungry. Keeping his eyes alert for predators that might be lurking nearby, he hopped to a large patch of meadow grass and ate breakfast.

The nearly silent sound of beating wings alerted him that an owl had settled in a tree not a stone's throw away. Chester shot lickety-split into a nearby hole.

"You don't let that lame leg slow you down, do you?" Snap said. "When you need to go fast, you can move and you're right to get out of the way."

The owl's fierce gaze met the soft strength of Snap's eyes. "Don't try it!" Snap's eyes said.

"She won't get me as long as you are around," Chester said, studying the owl's face.

"Learn from the deer," Snap advised. "When I'm after a deer and they feint right and dash left or the other way around . . . I find myself left with only a mouth full of grass."

"You settle down here in Powder River country . . . I wouldn't have to worry," Chester observed. "Living here is the best, don't you think?"

"Yeah, it's nice . . . You have everything a rabbit could want . . . but I have to . . . " Snap paused looking north toward the distant peaks of the Wallowa's. " . . . I know. I know there are wolves somewhere. I have to move on and find them."

"It's not fair . . . screech owls, eagles, big birds . . . cougars after us small ones all the time . . . we just eat weeds . . . it's not fair," Chester concluded, his voice trailing off.

"It's the way of the world . . . " Snap mused. "Remember, feint right and go left."

~ 7 ~

Meeting Burly

Snap peered back across the river for signs of Chester. The gangly, fearful critter was nowhere to be seen.

He crouched low behind a bush, paused a few moments and listened . . . no sound of bigs, which is what he called humans.

He began to think he had made the wrong decision. ' . . . Should I have listened to Chester,' he thought. ' . . . Nothing here . . . little water . . . nothing to eat . . . nothing here to want . . . certainly no wolves.'

'No big game around here either,' he thought. He

satisfied his hunger by catching and downing a batch of grasshoppers. They didn't taste good, but he could sustain himself by feeding on them until he encountered a deer.

Snap vacillated between thinking he should return to Powder River or move on in hope of finding a creek, a forest . . . other animals . . . anything promising a meaningful new life for a wolf. 'Or maybe I ought to just go back to the Imnaha . . . back to the pack . . . back to servitude?'

"No!" he shouted. "Over that wall is a place for me . . . with other wolves."

He got to his feet and continued south.

He came to a black rocky trail (the bigs call it a road) snaking its way over and through the rugged hills to the east and west. Snap had never seen a trail that busy. Hollowed out logs (the bigs call cars) raced this way and that. 'They can run faster than me. What are they looking for?' Snap wondered. It didn't look like they ever left the well-worn path. He crouched for a long while watching the strange creatures. He questioned whether he would ever be able to get across without being chased down.

He could see that the water channel passed into a black tunnel beneath the rock-trail. He'd never seen anything like this dark hole before. It could be a trap.

He inched forward into the gaping hole. The paws of the logs, pounding the trail surface above him made a terrible sound. As he dashed through the dark tube, he expected to be blown apart any second. He was relieved when he moved beyond the tunnel and on into the rolling hills to the south. It was not a trap after all.

An hour later, exhausted, he found a pile of straw to lie on. But first . . . he put his front paws on a mound of dirt near his bed, raised his nose, and howled.

He waited . . . No answer. The weary wolf stretched himself on the straw and fell asleep.

~~~

Snap woke at first light the following morning. A faint golden orange glow morphed into the inky darkness of the sky above him. It was beautiful.

'Flowers are like that too,' he thought. 'They start their lives out of darkness . . . open into midlife splendor of color and fade into gray at evening.' He wondered how it could be so . . . he wondered why it should be so. He would continue to wonder about things during the days ahead.

He got up, raised his nose to the air, and sniffed, hoping for the scent of wolves . . . no wolves . . . another whiff for any wildlife. Yes, ahead of him to the west, bears and deer roamed the forest.

He trotted into a patch of woods, caught, and devoured a young hare. The puny creature wouldn't supply him energy for very long, but it was better than worms or grasshoppers.
~~~

He trotted up and down varying grades of steepness, sometimes through the shade, and other times across bare red dirt strewn with sharp rocks.

He had traveled several miles through the undulating terrain, when he sensed a bear was nearby. He could handle any animal he might encounter . . . but he would rather not deal with a bear.

To challenge a bear was to test his fighting skills to their limits. He slowed his gate to reduce the sound his huge paws made. Snap knew that bears, like wolves, coyotes, bobcats and other sizable wild animals also have sensitive smell. He was glad the breeze was blowing from the west carrying the bear's scent to him and not the other way around. If he encountered the bear, he hoped it would be a cub . . . small enough not to be a threat.

It was not a cub. His keen eyes spotted a full-grown black bear swatting and eating grasshoppers with his big paws.

Snap stopped behind the mottled trunk of a tall pine and waited for the big bear to move on. Instead the huge creature raised his massive head, sniffed the air, and said, "I know you're there . . . smells like nothing I've ever smelled before. Are you bigger than I am? Come out where I can see you."

Snap had seen bears move. They can run fast, but Snap was sure he could run faster, if he needed to. He slowly crept from behind the tree, keeping a sharp eye on the bear.

"Oh," the bear said, "You're the biggest coyote I've ever seen. How did you get so big?"

"Why do you think I'm a coyote?"

The bear raised himself on his hind legs as if surprised at Snap's question. He wagged his enormous head.

"You look like a coyote . . . a big one . . . Only with bigger feet and there's something funny about your head."

Snap realized that the bear had never seen a wolf before . . . only coyotes and probably foxes and maybe guard dogs.

"I'm a wolf," Snap said, mincing his way a few steps toward the bear. "You've never seen a wolf before?"

"A wolf. Huh? What about wolves?" the big creature asked, tilting his head to the side.

"Wolves . . . We're just wolves, that's all. I'm Snap."

"I'm Burly . . . Burly Bear . . . to be exact."

"You've never seen a wolf? For sure?"

"Nope . . . never seen anything like you."

Snap took another relaxed step toward the big bear, feeling confident that Burly meant him no harm. "You know what's over there?" Snap asked, pointing a paw toward a mountain across a canyon.

"My cubs lumbering about with their mother," Burly answered.

"Anything else?"

"*Dooley Mountain* and some stone trails put there by bigs," Burly said matter-of-factly.

"And beyond that?" Snap asked, eyeing the range of mountains to the west.

"Don't know," Burly said, plopping another grasshopper into his mouth, " . . . Ever try one of these?

"Yeah, I eat 'em sometimes . . . when there's nothing better. Don't know what's there, huh?" Snap asked, anxious to hear something different. "Maybe wolves . . . you think?"

"Don't know, but if you want to find out, why don't you trot over and take a look?"

"You want to come?

"Lead the way," the big bear said, taking a step, " . . . it won't hurt to see what's over there."

~ 8 ~

More time with Burly Bear

"I smell deer," Snap told Burly. "I'm hungry . . . you eat deer?"

"If I can catch one . . . they're tricky . . . feint left and go right."

"Tricky is right," Snap agreed.

"I just as soon swat fish out of the river or gnaw on a wad of buckwheat," Burly continued.

"Listen," Snap said impatiently turning in a circle, " . . . I'll take the deer down . . . you can feed on the carrion."

While Snap trotted off light footed down a slope, Burly followed, placing one heavy paw after another to the ground and grunting with every step. The noise the big bear made annoyed Snap.

Suddenly, Snap stopped, his muscles tense. He spotted a doe partially hidden by a cluster of sagebrush a hundred yards away. Burly lumbered up beside Snap and snorted.

The deer's head shot up facing their direction, and before Snap could make a move, dashed away.

"Nice," Snap said sarcastically. "Do you have to move like a boulder?"

"Like a bear . . . " Burly said defensively. "What's wrong with the way I move?"

You scare everything else away . . . No wonder you have to eat hay and green stuff."

"You want to go on without me?" Burly asked, his tone revealing hurt feelings.

Snap looked at the big creature. He guessed the bear was right . . . he moved the best he could. Changing his tone, he said, "No, come on! Just try not to snort so much," and after a moment added, "Don't snort at all . . . would be best."

Burly didn't say anything. He just hurried to keep up, trying to make as little noise as possible. Snap felt certain that as long as the clumsy bear was with him, he was not likely to take a deer.

'Maybe I ought to ditch him,' he thought. 'No . . . he is a companion . . . haven't found a wolf . . . don't know when I will . . . '

By now the pair had hiked about five miles. Along the way Snap caught and devoured an ermine and a long-tailed weasel. They stopped for water a few miles south.

"Doesn't it bother you to eat those helpless little critters?" Burly asked, finishing off a leafy spurge and sitting down in the creek's cool water.

"Don't think about it . . . can't help it."

"Seems unfair," Burly said, " . . . big creature like you preying on the little ones . . . "

"Yeah, I guess . . . " Snap paused, reflecting, "But it's the way of the world . . . I noticed you pop grasshoppers and clean up after me . . . so who are you to judge."

"Have to get fat . . . get ready for hibernation . . . "

"Yeah," Snap said in Burly's face. "Let's get going."

"I need to rest a bit more," Burly said, getting out of the water.

Snap didn't like the idea of lingering . . . but he liked the bear's company so he settled down in the shade of a juniper until the moon showed over a ridge to the east.

Snap walked to a nearby rock outcropping and howled into the air. He waited for an answer. Again there was silence. Snap wondered if his quest was hopeless. Sleep overcame his thoughts.

~ 9 ~

Rusty Eagle at Sheep Mountain

The next morning Snap arose early, said goodbye to Burly and headed toward *Sheep Mountain.*

"Sheep Mountain . . . ought to be sheep here. A leg of lamb would taste good," he said out loud to himself. He spotted a vagrant shrew and a couple of long-tailed weasels but they were too quick for him. Finally, he caught a lethargic badger and made a tasty meal out of him.

He'd traveled about 15 miles when his aching feet told him it was time to rest. Besides that, he thought the banks of the *Malheur River* were a good place to stop for a couple of days. Snap stretched out on a big boulder and snoozed.

The sound of wings flapping nearby jarred him awake. He quickly sprang to his feet to protect himself from what he thought must be hungry vultures mistakenly thinking him a dead wolf. He didn't want the repulsive things pecking his eyes out.

"Up here," a voice said.

Snap looked up and there on a branch of a cottonwood tree sat Rusty Eagle — the enormous, friendly eagle known to animals throughout Oregon and beyond.

Snap had seen Rusty a year ago at a wolf roundup near *Hells Canyon*.

"You're Snap, aren't you?"

Snap was surprised that Rusty remembered him.

"Snap, yeah, sure, and you're Rusty . . . Rusty Eagle, right?"

"Yes, you got it."

"I can't believe it . . . How could you remember my name?"

"Easy," Rusty laughed. "You stand out, Snap. I am not surprised to find you hundreds of miles from home . . . You stand out."

"You were looking for me?"

"Not exactly. I was just returning home to *Umpqua National Forest* and saw you lounging here . . . thought I'd say hi and see how you're doing."

"You got good eyesight."

"Yes, it's the way of the world for us."

"Where you been?"

"The *Columbia River* . . . I go there often . . . fish and friends. Incidentally, I was at Imnaha only this morning."

"You were?" Snap asked excitedly.

"Yeah, saw your sisters and brothers. They're doing okay . . . looks like the boys will stay with the pack . . . happily subservient . . . you know."

"Yeah . . . I kinda wished I . . . " Snap drawled with a tone of nostalgia.

"You stand out, Snap," Rusty said cutting him off. "You're special! You did the right thing."

"How about mom? You didn't mention her."

"Your mom's fine . . . Oh, she calls for you every night . . . but she knows you can't come home."

"And Alpha?" Snap asked reluctantly.

"Your dad's good too . . . He's proud of you . . . the way of the world . . . the way of the wolf, you know."

"I wonder . . . " Snap said almost to himself.

"Haven't had any success finding other wolves, huh?"

"No. Found everything else, but no wolves."

"Not good," Rusty commiserated.

"Hey, you get around . . . you can spot a diamond on

a snake's back from hundreds of feet in the air. You must have seen wolves?"

"Yes, I've been all over . . . and in all my flights north, south, east and west, I've not seen a single wolf outside the Seven Devils . . . and the Wallowa's, of course."

Snap dropped his head in disappointment.

"That's not to say there aren't any . . . I've just not seen any. Despite my fine eyesight, I can't see everything. I might have missed . . . "

"Yeah, but . . . "

Rusty interrupted, "Wise Owl says wolves once roamed these forests . . . and still may . . . who knows?"

"Maybe I ought to go back to the Imnaha."

"Nothing there for you anymore. You've set your paw to this trail . . . your destiny lies ahead. You have to see where it leads."

~~~

Snap stood for a few seconds thinking about what had Rusty had said.

"What if I follow my destiny and I don't find another wolf?"

"There are no guarantees, but, like Wise Owl said, 'better to take the risk and have searched in vain, than to play it safe, and never have searched at all.'"

"I guess you're right . . . Wise Owl is right," Snap said. Then, satisfied that the way of the world for him was to keep going, he changed the subject. "Do you
~~~

know what's that way?" he asked, looking at a distant ridge to the south.

"You won't believe it," Rusty said brightly. "About five miles that way is the *Malheur Fork of Wolf Creek*," emphasizing the word "wolf."

"Really?" Snap asked excitedly.

"Really! Has to mean something."

"I was going to spend a couple of nights here, but five miles isn't far," Snap said. "There is still plenty of daylight left . . . think I'll head out for *Wolf Mountain* and rest there."

"I'm glad you've resolved to continue your quest," Rusty said cheerily, "And I must continue mine . . . reaching Umpqua before nightfall . . . good to see you. If you get to my part of the woods, I want to see you . . . you hear?"

Rusty lifted himself into the air and flew off in a westerly direction.

Ready to scale the hill in front of him, Snap watched him go.

~ 10 ~

To Wolf Mountain

"Tassspt, tassspt, tassspt," Snap heard coming from water's edge. He looked at his feet. There looking at him with bulging eyes was a western toad.

"Tassspt, tassspt, tassspt," the toad repeated.

"You say something to me you want me to understand, you'll have to talk wolf . . . well, at least speak animal," Snap growled.

"I got a beetle wing stuck in my throat," the toad said, hopping up to Snap.

"You going to be okay?" Snap asked. He'd seen frogs before . . . but none like this one. The toad's back was a dusky greenish color with red and black blotchy bumps peppering the surface. Two eyes bulged on top of its head.

Its wide mouth was cast in what appeared, to Snap, like an ear-to-ear smile. It had three toes on each of its four legs.

"I will be okay, if you give me a ride," the toad said in a raspy voice.

"Give you a ride? Why should I give you a ride? Where you going?"

"Heard the big bird mention Wolf Mountain. I gotta go there."

"So go! I'm not stopping you."

"Five miles is a long way for a western toad . . . think about it . . . how long it will take me to walk five miles . . . Wolf Mountain . . . that's what I heard the eagle say."

"I can see it would take you a long time to walk one mile, never mind five . . . I doubt if you could walk that far in a year."

"You see . . . but it wouldn't take long, if you'd give me a ride on your back."

"Why would you want to go so far away from where you live? You may not be able to return."

"It's something I have to do . . . it's in my gut . . . I have to do it . . . " the toad burped.

"Oh," Snap said thinking of his own plight. "What's your name?"

"Bulge. Bulge Toad."

"Well, Bulge, climb aboard and let's get going."

Bulge sprang into action. He grabbed Snap's tail with the three fingers on his front legs, then, grasping fur with the toes of his rear legs, he scrambled onto Snap's back. "Ready!" he shouted.

With that, Snap bounded across the creek and up a hill. The new friends were on their way to Wolf Mountain.

~~~

The ride was a bumpy shakeup for Bulge. His fingers gripped the wolf's thick fur with tenacious determination.

"Da . . . da . . . do we ha . . . have . . . ta . . . to go so fa . . . fast?" the desperate toad yelled, holding on with all his might.

"Gotta find out," Snap said, jumping over a large rock in the middle of Wolf Creek and coming down to splash water over himself and his nervous passenger.

"Wa . . . wa . . . water fe . . . els go . . . ood."

"Yeah," Snap said.

He bounded onto the creek bank and into a sparse stand of juniper, over a bed of wild flowers, and back into and out of the creek.

Snap slowed to a trot, then to a walk, and finally stopped. He gazed at the mountain in front of him.
~~~

"Why'd we stop?" Bulge asked, " . . . we here?"

"Yeah, we're here," Snap answered, showing his disappointment.

Bulge hopped off Snap's back onto a spread of orange dirt nurturing a clump of yellow bladder-pod. "Guess I can find my clan from here, then," he said, making his way toward the trickling waters of Wolf Creek. "Thanks for the ride."

"Look at that," Snap said, ignoring Bulge's words.

" . . . Thanks for the ride," Bulge repeated, squatting waist deep in water.

"Ride?" Snap answered absentmindedly.

"Yeah, the ride . . . " Bulge said, "or, I should say, the dust-devil run we just went on."

"Oh, I was thinking about Wolf Mountain . . . forgot you were there."

"Doesn't look like much of a mountain to me," Bulge said.

"Me either. That's the problem . . . it's like a bump on a hill."

"Yeah, like one of the blotchy bumps on my back," Bulge croaked, enjoying his cleverness.

Snap didn't laugh. "No self-respecting wolf would hang out here," he complained. Lifting his nose into the sky, he emitted a long howl that reverberated across the valley and returned as a mournful echo.

Bulge shivered and bleeped.

"Shush!" Snap barked.

Bulge pursed his lips and rolled the dome shaped eyes atop his head.

"No answer . . . didn't think there would be," Snap concluded.

Bulge, walked into the water, swam to and mounted a rock near the center of the stream. "Hope you find your kind. Mine will be squatting around here somewhere. I'm off to find them. Thanks again for the hair-raising lift."

"Hair-raising lift . . . that's rich coming from a hairless toad."

~ 11 ~

The porcupine standoff

Snap, who was tired and sore from the five-mile dash he'd just endured, settled under the shade of a pine tree and quickly fell asleep. When he awakened, he trotted to the creek for water.

Lap, lap, lap, lap, . . . the water took away the cottony feeling in his mouth. Then, munch, munch, munch, he heard coming from the cluster of paintbrush behind him. His muscles tensed.

"Is that you Bulge?" he called, turning to look.

The munching stopped. Snap couldn't see an origin for the sound.

"Bulge?"

"Not likely," a prickly voice came, "I don't know what a bulge is."

Snap strolled through the purple foliage looking for the owner of the voice . . . nothing.

"You look like a giant coyote . . . the biggest I've ever seen," the surly voice said.

Snap looked up. Sitting in the forked branches of a big cottonwood sat a portly porcupine looking down on him.

"Coyote . . . " Snap laughed. "Not likely," he continued mocking the porcupine's words and tone. "I'm a wolf. Snap's my name. What's yours?"

"Well, wolf, nobody invited you, I'll bet! What are you doing here?"

"Minding my own business, if it's any business of yours!"

"I'm not afraid of you . . . you may be big, but I'm not afraid," the porcupine growled.

"Really?" Snap said, annoyed and warned, "You need to know that I dine on characters like you."

"Not likely! You're not a fisher," the porcupine said, extending her quills into a threatening stance.

Her challenge defused Snap's bravado. "I see what you mean. I'll keep my distance and hope you'll keep yours."

"Now that we understand each other, you can answer my question . . . I asked you what you are doing here?"

"And you didn't answer my question . . . what's your name?" Snap asked.

"You go first," the porcupine demanded.

"I asked first," Snap returned, toying with the stubborn porcupine.

"Stabby!" the porcupine snapped and settled her quills to their resting position.

"Seems apropos," and before Stabby could complain, he added, "I'm looking for wolves . . . a pack of wolves to be exact."

"Only things around here like you are coyotes . . . plenty of those . . . but nothing as big as you . . . well, bears maybe and deer . . . and elk."

"Elk!" Snap gushed, "Yeah, I can smell them . . . you know where they are?"

Suspicious, Stabby asked, "Why do you want to know?"

"Ah . . . for a wolf to bring down an elk is a long time feast. It's the way of the world for wolves."

"Yeah," Stabby agreed and lamented, "like it's the way of the world for fishers to feast on us."

"There you have it . . . look at you . . . eating its bark . . . killing that tree . . . it is the way of the world," he paused to let his words sink in, then pleaded " . . . so help me find the elk."

"There's a herd of them that hang out over there on *Jump-off-Joe Mountain*," Stabby said, climbing down from the tree and pointing her nose northwest. "But those fellows are huge. They have antlers as big as trees . . . you going to take them on alone. Good luck with that."

"You're right, it takes a pack of wolves to bring down an elk . . . but I'm alone . . . so what choice do I have?"

"You could go after something smaller like a mule deer fawn for starters," Stabby pointed out.

"Might do that too, but I'm aiming to be an alpha wolf . . . means I have to take chances . . . I have to learn to lead."

"Learn? Who's going to teach you?"

"Teach myself . . . " Snap answered. "Over there, you say?"

"That's what I hear," Stabby said. "Listen, I'm usually out at night . . . sleep in the day. I'm going back to bed."

"Thanks for the tip . . . you're not so prickly as I first thought."

"Get out! I'm supposed to be abrasive . . . It's my nature."

"The way of the world, huh?"

"The way of the world," Stabby repeated, "If you get back this way, I'm holed up in that rotten log over there." She waddled through the paintbrush toward the fallen tree.

Snap turned and trotted over the summit of Wolf Mountain northwest toward Jump-off-Joe Mountain.

~ 12 ~

Finding elk at Jump-off-Joe Mountain

It was noon by the time Snap reached the lower elevation of Jump-off-Joe Mountain. The scent of elk permeated the air.

He headed southwest where he could get downwind of the herd, crouched low in the bunchgrass, and crept toward them.

Low . . . crouching . . . sneak . . . stop . . . Low . . . crouching sneak . . . stop . . . Low . . . crouching . . . sneak . . . STOP.

Stabby's warning rang in his head. The wisest course of action for him would be to withdraw from this scene to find a herd of deer. That would be the easiest thing to do. That would be what a subordinate wolf would do, but not an alpha . . . well, not this alpha.

When Snap saw that it was a good time to make his move, he sprang into action and dashed into the open. The sudden sound and the appearance of a large wolf coming at them startled the elk.

The cow began running down the steep grade into the canyon separating Jump-off Joe Mountain from Wolf Mountain.

He dodged a sagebrush bush and lunged at her rear leg. His first attempt missed. His chest hit a bush as he came down.

His agile body quickly recovered and he was at her heels once more. He was ready to lunge, when he became conscious of a dangerous bull elk thundering his direction.

He knew if he abandoned his chase, he could easily escape the bull's charge. But doing so would cost him his mark.

As Snap brought her down, suddenly the wind was knocked out of him from the impact of the bull's antlers.

The force of the hit sent Snap sailing through the air. He landed in sagebrush.

Sharp pains gripped his stomach and ribs . . . almost too painful to move.

Snap's huge paws gripped the branches of the sage and thrust him off the bush. When his feet hit the ground, he sprang into a run toward the rounded top of Jump-off-Joe Mountain and disappeared among the sagebrush, juniper, and scrub pine.

The bull followed . . . and then, stopped, snorted into the air, turned, and trotted away.

Snap found a spot under a pine to stop, to nurse his wounds and plan his next move. As he listened to the distant sound of the western peewee, the rasping of grasshopper wings, and the se-lip, cherp, treep of a dusky flycatcher, the sun sunk low in the west.

A chill settled over the terrain. Snap was hungry and terribly thirsty. He needed to get to water and get to the downed cow.

He struggled to his feet fighting less stiffness and pain than he expected and followed the drag marks until he found her. Several coyotes had finished his job and were now feasting on the carcass.

Snap didn't feel much like getting into a fight with a pack of coyotes but he had brought the cow down . . . it was his prize . . . he was determined to claim his prey.

He stiffened his muscles, raised his nose into the air, and sent a painful, but terrible, howl into the afternoon sky. Then, he slowly walked into the open.

The coyotes were stunned by the sound they had just heard, and now at what they saw. For the past few nights they had heard the wolf's cry far off in the distance, but not this close.

They had never seen a wolf. His size was intimidating. He would make two or three of the biggest of them.

The leader of the coyote pack said something to the others, and then trotted away down the slope and into the canyon below. The others followed.

Snap walked to the carrion and began eating. Overhead, vultures circled waiting their turn and a marten, a wolverine, and a badger watched from the underbrush.

Once satisfied, he walked away. Before he settled in, he sent a howl into the night. He waited for a recognizable response. None came.

~ 13 ~

Meeting the coyote

Snap awoke to the early morning sun slicing through the sparse branches of his juniper cover. He'd eaten well the day before.

When he returned to yesterday's carcass, he found that the scavengers had left only the bones. He crushed several with his powerful teeth, and sucked out the nourishing bone marrow.

Feeling satisfied, he sniffed the air and resumed his journey. As he trotted further south, Snap noticed the trees and the understory were thinning out, and grass was giving way to larger and larger patches of barren dirt. The sun seemed to be getting hotter.

~~~

After a brief rest in the sparse shade of a juniper, Snap rose to his feet and trotted off into the barren landscape. Late in the day as the sun neared the western horizon, Snap found himself on a brush-covered hill. It was a suitable place to find shelter for the night.

He stood at the apex of the ridges and performed his customary ritual of sending a full-throated howl into the graying sky and waiting for a response. He was surprised to hear an answer . . . only it wasn't a wolf's howl. It was a coyote and it came from a knoll not far away.

Snap growled quietly in the direction of the coyote. A soft bark came in response. It appeared that the coyote wanted to approach him. Snap wondered why.

Wolves and coyotes are natural competitors, if not enemies. Unless the wolf is injured or sick, the larger animal always has the advantage. A single coyote would never challenge a healthy wolf.

Snap suspected the coyote was not alone. If there were a pack of coyotes, Snap would likely have to defend himself. He hadn't fully recovered from his encounter with the elk, but should the coyotes attack, he would do what was necessary to protect himself.

"You brought down a cow elk," a voice said.
~~~

Snap was surprised that a coyote, which had witnessed his encounter with the elk, had the courage to follow him.

"Who are you?" Snap growled suspiciously.

"Tag. I'm Tag Coyote," the voice said.

"Is that your name?" Snap asked.

"Tag . . . yeah, Tag."

"So . . . Tag, you alone?"

"Yeah, came by myself."

"How do I know that?" Snap asked guardedly, "Come out where I can see you."

Tag slid from behind a sagebrush bush and stopped, arrested by Snap's severe gaze.

Though dusk was settling over the terrain, Snap could make out the tell-tail color markings of the coyote.

"What are you doing here . . . away from your pack?" Snap asked bewildered. He moved menacingly toward the young coyote and demanded, "Why are you alone?"

Tag backed away, crouching in a subservient position. "I sneaked away last night and followed you all day."

"Why would you do that?"

"You faced the elk herd and took down the cow by yourself," Tag said admiringly.

"I just did what I had to do . . . Look, you need to go back to your pack."

"I don't want to . . . I want to follow you . . . to learn from you," Tag pleaded.

"It makes sense for a wolf to leave his pack . . . go out on his own . . . he's supposed to . . . he has to . . . It's the way of the wolf. But a coyote?"

"I don't know about other coyotes . . . I just know I want to follow you."

"I'm looking for wolf pack . . . " Snap explained. "You think you can help me find one?"

"I can try . . . I have a better nose than anyone in my pack, and I can see things the others can't see," Tag bragged.

Snap laughed a gentle wolf's laugh. "Better smeller and better lookers, huh?"

"Yeah, and I can out-run them all."

"If you are quiet, you can bed down with me for the night," Snap said.

Tag followed him.

When the wolf and the coyote had their sleeping spaces ready, Snap turned to Tag, bringing a huge paw down on his shoulder.

"But, if you fooled me . . . if you are trying to fool me . . . if your den of coyotes are out there waiting to attack me, you'll need to run faster than anything you've ever seen 'cause I'll run you down and . . . "

"No more coyotes! No more coyotes," Tag assured.

"Better not be!" Snap warned. "Alright then, let's quiet down . . . get some sleep."

Tag curled up in a ball on his bed of straw. Snap rose from his, walked to the apex of his hill, and raised his voice into the night. He awaited the hoped for response. Nothing.

Tag crawled from the bed, climbed onto the mound near Snap, and emitted a high-pitched coyote howl. Almost immediately, from the remote distance came an answering coyote call.

"Ah yes, of course," Snap breathed, "there are coyotes in these mountains . . . but no wolves." He turned to Tag and warned, "They better not come looking for you!" He paused and after reflection added, "It's better you go back to them, tomorrow."

"I'm not leaving! Not if I can help it."

"In the morning you may have to," Snap said " . . . now, let's be quiet."

~ 14 ~

Teaming up with Tag

The next morning, when Snap awakened, he saw no sign of Tag. 'Good,' he thought, 'the young pup is on his way back to the others.'

He gazed west. His nose picked up the scent of freshly killed prey. He was surprised to find a dead rabbit, a lazuli bunting, and a small pile of prickly pear lying near a sage bush.

He knew that the meal didn't just conveniently show up. Something had to put it there, and would expect it to be there when it returned. Of course, he hoped it was a wolf.

Snap consumed the remains of the rabbit, and was sniffing at the lazuli bunting, when he heard something coming toward him. His muscles stiffened ready to defend, if necessary. He was surprised to see Tag bounding up with a long-tailed weasel dangling from his mouth. Tag plopped the catch on the ground in front of Snap and sat back on his haunches, looking proud and satisfied.

Snap was speechless.

Tag broke the silence, "What do you think?"

"Well, I'll be the son of an alpha. You've been busy! I thought you decided to go back to your pack."

"Not me. I'm doing my part . . . helping us get to . . . " he paused, not knowing what came next, then, plunged on " . . . helping us get to wherever it is we are going." He bit into the bunting and shook it, causing feathers to fly in all directions.

"I'll give it to you . . . you're persistent," Snap admitted. "I told you, I'm looking for other wolves . . . You'll be out of place when I find them, don't you think?"

"You haven't found them yet, and I want to find out what it's like to be a wolf."

"That's funny . . . kind of a silly pipe dream."

"Maybe your dream is too . . . You ever think of that?" Tag challenged.

"Alright, you win," Snap conceded, "You can tag along."

"I knew it," Tag said, "I thought you'd like breakfast brought right to your nose."

"It was a good move on your part," Snap laughed, " . . . but you don't have to do that. I'm a perfectly capable hunter, you know."

"Yeah, I know. Remember, I saw you challenge that bull elk to bring down that cow . . . that was something!"

"And I don't like bird."

"You don't?" Tag asked unbelieving.

"And I don't eat fruit," Snap stated, nudging the cactus fruit with his paw.

"You're kidding."

"And if you really want to know the truth, I'm not really that fond of rabbit."

"Oh . . . " Tag sighed and conceded, "Rabbits and other smalls is all I can do . . . I can't take on a deer by myself . . . like you." Then, he said excitedly, " . . . but I can help you bring down an elk . . . " And after another pause he looked at Snap admiringly and said, " . . . even though you don't need my help."

"Okay, we're a team . . . Now, let's get going," Snap said, and started to trot away.

"Wait a minute!" Tag called, "I gotta clean up this weasel . . . you had your breakfast . . . let me grab a couple of bites."

Snap didn't say anything . . . just sat on his haunches, waiting for his young coyote friend to eat.

"Couple of prickly pear . . . and I'm with you," Tag said, devouring the ripe fruit.

A moment later Tag was at Snap's side. "You don't like prickly pear? That's not good. They're like a topping on the feast . . . dessert you might say."

"I'd eat the awful things if I had to . . . but wouldn't like it," Snap conceded.

The two friends headed across a barren stretch of rust colored dirt, scattered rocks, and sparse patches of sagebrush.

The sun continued, unloading its searing heat on the dry open terrain and the creatures that exist in the sage-brush country of *Central Oregon*.

At sunset the alpha wolf and the coyote raised their voices into the night, sending howls across the prairie. They solemnly waited for answers. None came.

~ 15 ~

Heading to snow country

The morning sun rose again to shine on the lone wolf and the trusting coyote.

Snap had traveled hundreds of miles, making friends with many animals along the way, but he had not found another wolf. He was discouraged.

'A subordinate would go back, but I can't do that,' he thought. 'I can't act like a subordinate again . . . No, I have to act like an alpha!'

Then, turning to Tag he said, "No, I have to be an alpha."

"You are," Tag responded matter-of-factly, not knowing why Snap said what he just said.

Snap turned his gaze south to open spaces where the terrain looked to be even more dry and stark. He wanted to get Tag's opinion about where to go next, but knew the 'yes' coyote would grin and say, "Where you go, I go."

Half to himself and without thinking, Snap asked, "Which way should we go?"

"This way," Tag said, trotting off in a westerly direction.

"Who's the alpha?" Snap asked, catching up.

Shortly, the two friends came upon a hard-rock trail. They carefully crouched behind some bitterbrush and waited for several cars to speed past.

When Tag saw that nothing was coming from either direction, he shouted, "Let's go," and scampered from behind his hideout and across the wide trail.

They didn't stop running until they were safely away.

That evening they challenged the quietness by howling wolf and coyote calls into the night. Yes, coyotes answered, but no wolves. Snap asked Tag why he didn't leave and join the coyotes.

"They're not alpha wolves," Tag answered, as if no other explanation were needed.

~~~

The next morning, Snap decided he and Tag would head for the snow-covered mountains to the west.
~~~

By mid-afternoon Tag's legs felt like lead. "I'm done. I can't go on," he said weakly.

Snap stopped, circled a couple of times, and returned to face him. "You're not done. You want to be an alpha coyote?" He didn't wait for an answer, "Get up and get moving!"

Tag groaned his pain. He staggered to his feet and continued dragging himself through the heat.

Snap looked at the desert lying before them. He knew that if they didn't pick up their pace, they would never make it far enough to find relief in the snow covered mountains that lay before them.

The mountains grew closer and closer and higher and higher.

"Listen to this," he said moving into a gentle trot. He began to sing, "Water and food lie just ahead . . . Stopping here is to be like dead." He turned his head to see how Tag was responding. The gangly coyote was struggling to match Snap's walking gate.

"'That's the spirit that'll keep you alive,'" Snap sang, "'Paw after paw with an alpha's drive.' Come on sing it," Snap urged and repeated, "Water and food lie just ahead."

Tag joined Snap with . . . "and food lie just ahead."

"That's it! Let's keep it up and we'll be there before you know it. 'Water and food lie just ahead . . . colors of a rainbow without the red.'"

The wolf and the coyote continued singing the survival song. Snap gradually picked up the pace to a steady gentle trot.

When the setting sun touched the top of *Paulina Peak*, the exhausted pair stopped for the night. A meager pool of water saved them from deadly dehydration. Immediately, Tag dropped on a bed of bunchgrass and fell asleep.

Snap howled a new howl into the night. He wished his mother could hear him. He waited an answering call . . . but none came.

~ 16 ~

Danger at Hole-in-the-Ground

The morning sky was clear . . . the air was dry. The orange sun was ready to threaten the lone wolf and coyote.

"We are heading for water . . . I can smell it," Snap said to his companion. "Let's get going."

"And food?" the famished coyote returned.

"And food," Snap encouraged, though not certain what they would find.

Snap's senses were right. The forests in the *Cascade Mountains* began in earnest with trees, water, animals, and birds of every sort.

"Wouldn't this be a good place to stay?" Tag asked.

"Maybe . . . " Snap hesitated, his urge to find a wolf pack gnawing at him. "Maybe for you . . . " he continued, "Coyotes in these mountains, but no wolves."

~~~

By late afternoon, the two runners reached *Hole-in-the-Ground.* They found themselves looking over a vast bowl with nothing at the bottom but what looked like a pocket of muddy water.

It appeared that rain and snow seldom reached the huge pit. If they had, there would be a lake instead of a huge dry pocket.

The adventurers trotted down into the pit. A bullet riddled barrel sat in the shallow mud puddle at the center of the crater. When he was a pup, Snap had seen the effect of bullets from the big's guns, or as he called them—fire spitting sticks.

"The fire from those sticks that spit will go right through you," Alpha Wolf had cautioned. He had commanded them to stay away from places where they were found.

"We'd better get out of here," Snap said, surveying in all directions the distant rim of Hole-in-the-Ground.

Tag followed Snap's gaze. "There's a trail coming down
~~~

that way," Tag said, pointing to the dirt path descending from the northern crest.

"Then let's go this way," Snap said, dashing off to the west.

Soon the pair neared the western rim of the dry lake.

Suddenly, Snap heard a zinging sound followed by a crack. A spurt of dirt jumped up in front of him, followed by another. The second stung his left ear and buried itself in the trunk of a juniper in front of him.

"Run for your life!" Snap shouted and dashed, zig-zagging his way up to the western crest of the hill. Tag followed Snap as best he could, but his legs weren't long enough to keep up. Bullets split the air around them and above their heads.

Snap reached the crest of the hill, crossed it and hurried down its outer side into a grove of trees. He crouched cautiously on the ground and waited for Tag to join him. Tag did not come.

Snap knew he dared not return to look for him. To show himself now at the rim of the lake would be suicide. He was torn between the need to protect himself by staying hidden, and his desire to help Tag get to safety.

He paced back and forth, hoping Tag would appear at any moment, but the coyote didn't come. He hoped Tag had found a place to hide.

He lay uneasily in his hiding place and waited for darkness. Since wolves can travel just fine at night, he would search when it got dark . . . for now he felt he must stay out of sight.

As darkness fell, Snap crept from beneath his hiding place and howled into the night. He heard the sound of a lone coyote. It was Tag.

Snap howled a joyful call. The answering cry that pierced the night was packed with stress. Snap called again to reassure Tag that he was on his way to find him.

The moonless night grew darker. Snap would not let this be a barrier to getting to Tag. He moved stealthily among the trees and bushes across barren fields and up the hill.

On the crest of the crater he found Tag lying beneath a juniper licking the fleshy part of his thigh where a bullet had passed though.

The darkness prevented Snap from getting a clear look at the wound. "The bigs may come again when the sun comes up . . . can you walk?"

"It hurts . . . but I can hop," Tag said weakly.

"And drag, I'd say," Snap added.

"Yeah, I was afraid they would come find me and . . . " Tag said, his voice trailing off.

"Yeah, lucky they didn't."

"We have to get away from here before morning," Snap urged.

"I'll try."

"A little way at a time," Snap encouraged, "if that's what it takes. Come on, let's go."

In the dark the two friends slowly made their way toward Snap's hiding place.

He'd howled to find Tag . . . he'd not call again tonight. Sleep took his mind.

~ 17 ~

Rescuing Tag

When first light glowed in the eastern sky, Snap nuzzled Tag. "We have to leave here . . . too close to Hole-in-the-Ground."

Tag struggled to his feet. He hurt but he didn't complain.

It was still dark as they prepared to cross the big trail. They were startled by the appearance of two huge yellow eyes rapidly coming at them.

Tag thought the eyes were looking for him. He turned and limped a few paces back into the sagebrush.

"Here! Stay here!" Snap shouted. "Don't let them see you move. Quick, under this tree."

Tag was frightened. He'd already had one deadly encounter with bigs yesterday. He was torn between running away from the yellow eyes and listening to the alpha wolf. The thought of being alone in this hostile terrain motivated him to quickly hop back to join Snap, who was already out of sight under a juniper.

Tag crawled in beside Snap. They lay flat on the ground beneath the tree, avoiding the gaze of the oncoming log. Soon, the big eyes swept past them, making a roaring, growling sound as they did. The two small red eyes rapidly disappeared into the still dark morning.

All was quiet once again.

"Let's get across and into that grove before more yellow eyes come," Snap said, stepping out onto the hard trail's black surface.

Tag hopped across and into the grass on the other side.

Snap caught a pair of rabbits and brought one to Tag, who had settled under the low branches of a pine. He resisted the urge to howl for fear his call would attract bigs camping near the Hole.

~~~

It was cold the following night when the pair arrived at *Scott Mountain* a couple of miles east of *Crater Lake.* Temperatures at theses altitudes were telling the wolf and the coyote that winter was arriving.
~~~

At the western foot of the mountain, Snap and Tag settled into a comfortable pocket in a clump of boulders piled on the side of a cliff. The shelter kept them out of the sharp wind.

Tag's leg was recovering.

"I'm back to my old self," he said, dropping a blue grouse at the big wolf's feet.

"Argh," Snap moaned. "You know I don't like birds . . . feathers, argh."

"Better than nothing," Tag said, chomping into the lifeless bird.

"I'm not so sure. These woods are full of good stuff. I'm holding out for fur . . . I'll bring something down tomorrow."

"It's okay with me," Tag said, gulping down the last of the grouse.

Before curling into his sleeping spot, Snap climbed onto a downed tree and howled into the crisp mountain air. Without waiting for a response, he settled down for the night.

Tag took the same log and howled as loudly as he could and was surprised when the returning howl was nearby. Standing in the semi darkness in a patch of sorrel was a pair of female coyotes.

~~~

"Yeah, we heard a coyote. It was you, wasn't it?" one of the coyotes asked.

"Yeah . . . probably," Tag answered.
~~~

"But we heard a dog too . . . can't be sure about dogs . . . don't want to mess with dogs . . . You alone?"

Tag moved closer. "Not alone, but you don't have to worry about Snap. He's not a dog . . . he's a wolf, and he likes coyotes."

"Not so fast," Snap said, emerging from his bed.

The two strangers eyes popped at his size. They turned tail, dashed across the opening and into a stand of underbrush.

"You'll get no harm from me," Snap called to the retreating coyotes, "I'm looking for wolves, that's all. Do you know? Are there wolves in these forests?"

Becky and Lillie carefully emerged from the understory.

Keeping her distance Becky said, "I've never seen anything like you before. You're big . . . too big . . . Aren't you afraid?"

"Not me," Tag answered. "Snap's been good to me. He just wants to find wolves."

"Nothing like you, here," Lillie added, still eying Snap.

"You two can come with us," Tag said admiringly to the two good-looking lady coyotes.

"Go with a dog? Are you crazy?" Becky exclaimed.

"He's not a dog. He's a wolf."

"Whatever . . . he better stay away from us," Lillie said, baring her teeth.

"No! No need to snarl at Snap," Tag said, "He won't hurt you."

"Whatever he is, he's new to me and I'm not taking a chance," Becky said, trotting away toward the underbrush.

"Me neither," Lillie said, quickly following her sister out of harm's way.

The sisters disappeared.

"Hey! You're wrong about Snap," Tag called after them, not knowing where they had gone.

Snap chuckled, "So much for friendly howls into the night."

"Yeah, howls are supposed to bring coyotes together . . . they're cute . . . you think?"

Snap chuckled again. "Well, not exactly . . . well, the brazen one . . . a little . . . I can see why they appeal to you. You might want to stay here with them . . . think about it . . . I'm going to sleep."

Tag nervously paced the clearing thinking about what it would mean for him to settle here with the coyote sisters. The night got colder and colder but the chill didn't bother him. He was engrossed in thought.

Tag knew he would not be continuing on with Snap. He knew he would stay with the coyote sisters instead. He also knew that Snap had no choice but to move on in his relentless search for other wolves . . . for a mate. He wished his friend well.

Finally, he gave into weariness and joined Snap in the temporary den. After an hour he was overcome by fatigue and fell asleep.

~ 18~

Crater Lake

Alone once more, Snap trudged through the deepening snow following *Bear Creek* toward the deep blue waters of Crater Lake. He found a cliff overhang with no snow beneath it. He pawed leaves and needles into a resting pad and laid down.

His breath came in short white snorts, marking the air from his nostrils. Snap's thick fur coat protected him against the icy winds. He lay in his protected shelter watching the snowflakes shooting in front of him at sharp angles. Their repetitive movement was hypnotic. He felt warm and secure.

When the storm let up, he would continue his journey into the unknown looking for his mate . . . until then, a fantastic world of swirling snowflakes danced before him.

Snap thought about Tag. He missed the friendly coyote's carefree manner . . . his optimistic outlook. He wished the wily coyote had come with him.

A puff of wind sent a cluster of snowflakes into his face. He crawled to the mound of snow piling up outside his cave. The distinct odor of skunk permeated the air.

'I wonder if this critter is lost or maybe a brave adventurer like me,' he thought.

As he entered a stand of pine, he came face to face with it. He stopped abruptly, not wanting set off its protective system.

"Whoa," he said, "Save your ammunition . . . I'll just skirt around you . . . and be on my way."

"Hold it!" the skunk shouted, "I'm out of my element . . . give me a ride and I'll not riddle you with my perfume . . . try to get by and you'll get a fur full."

"Nah . . . you wouldn't do that," the unbelieving wolf said.

"I'm desperate!" the lost skunk retorted, turning to aim his weapon directly at Snap. "The snow is getting too deep for me . . . I can't keep wading . . . " His voice trailed off into a whimper.

"What's your name . . . where're you headed?" Snap asked, stalling for time while his mind scrambled for a means of escape.

"I'm Squirt. Squirt Skunk. I'm headed for a lower elevation . . . This high up . . . getting through the snow is hard for skunks."

"Hard for wolves too, but we tough it out . . . "

"Well, I can't tough it out. I'll die, if I don't get out of it."

"Why'd you come up too high in the first place?"

"Curiosity. Stupid curiosity . . . You know what that is, I'll bet. You don't look like you belong here either."

Snap thought, 'The skunk is right . . . curiosity is what got me so far from the Imnaha Valley . . . well, curiosity . . . and the primal urge.'

"You're right," he admitted, " . . . I don't belong here . . . but I've come a long way to get here . . . I'm looking for other wolves like me," he paused, hoping for the answer he needed, but fearing what he was about to hear, "None here, huh?"

"Pesky coyotes, vicious cougars, terrible lynx, grabby hawks, eager eagles, and other carnivores, but I've never seen one like you," Squirt said, his teeth chattering. "Now, how about it . . . how about a lift down the mountain."

Other small animals had hitched rides and toting one more wasn't a problem . . . Though Snap didn't like the idea of being threatened, the idea of being shot in the nose with skunk perfume prevented him from moving.

He was about to say something when Squirt turned to face him and whimpered, "Ah . . . I can't do it. You didn't do anything to me . . . I'm not going to squirt you . . . I can't. I just want to get safely down the mountain."

"I'm glad you won't squirt me . . . but I'm not sure you want to go with me . . . I'm following the high-up crest of the mountain first . . . lots of snow all the way, I imagine."

"I'll take my chances . . . can't stay here. You okay with hauling me?" Squirt asked.

"I've done it before," Snap responded, " . . . Well, not a skunk," he went on, " . . . but others wanting a ride. Okay, okay, let's get going."

Squirt scooted to a nearby log, climbed on it, and then hopped onto Snap's back. Snap trotted off along the trail with his passenger clinging to the fur on his neck. It was a funny sight to see a gray wolf loping over a carpet of white snow with a white-striped black skunk straddling his back.

"You always smell like a skunk?" Snap asked, trying not to breathe Squirt's aroma too deeply.

"I guess I'm used to it . . . doesn't bother us skunks . . . it's the way we protect ourselves . . . sorry."

Snap trudged through the snow into mid-afternoon, when exhaustion forced him to rest into a bed of needles under low hanging bows of a giant fir.

Squirt hopped from his back, scoured the fir branches for bugs, and then caught a mouse napping under a fir cone. He gathered up a mouthful of bugs and laid them in front of Snap to repay the big wolf for transporting him through the heavy layers of snow.

At dusk the pair had reached *Willow Lake* where Snap brought down a straggling deer. After eating their fill, they settled down for the night.

Of course, Snap howled into the night . . . he heard coyotes, but no wolves among them.

~ 19 ~

Alone again

Early the next morning Snap crawled from his niche in the rock fortress into the cold mountain air. He was disappointed that there was no sign of the skunk, but in a way, he understood. Squirt was safely out of the deep snow and there was no need to stay with Snap. He called to him anyway, just to make sure. There was no answer.

Though he was beginning to believe that he would never find wolves, the primal urge drove him on. "I'm an alpha wolf. I will find wolves."

~~~
~~~

He'd trudged two miles when suddenly the silence was broken by a rasping kack-kack-kacking noise. He looked up to see a peregrine falcon perched on a bare limb near the top of an alder.

"What're you looking for that way?" the falcon asked.

"To find a wolf pack," Snap said. "Who are you? What's your name?"

"Harlena. Harlena Gwin Falcon . . . "

"Harlena," Snap said.

"Harlena Gwin Falcon," Harlena interrupted.

"Harlena Gwin," Snap repeated, letting the name roll off his long tongue.

"Falcon . . . Harlena Gwin Falcon."

"Harlena . . . Gwin . . . Falcon," Snap articulated, "I got it . . . and I'm Snap."

"Snap," Harlena Gwin Falcon said, expecting more.

"Wolf! Snap Wolf," Snap clarified, in hopes the matter was settled.

"Snap Wolf . . . Wolf, I've never . . . "

Snap interrupted, "I know . . . you've never seen anything like me before . . . and don't know anything about Wallowa . . . which means that as far as you know, there are no wolves living in this part of the forest . . . right?"

"Oh," the falcon said confused . . . then, innocently asked, "If you've never been here, how do you know wolves don't live here?"

"You just told me you've never seen a wolf before,"

Snap said, perplexed. "Never mind. You can fly high above everything, so you know what I'll likely find if I go that way," Snap concluded, pointing his nose south.

"That way?" Harlena Gwin Falcon quizzed, tilting her head in a southerly direction. "Hah, that way you'll find forests with trees, creeks, lakes, hills and mountains, but I don't know about wolves . . . "

"Trees, creeks, lakes, bushes and flowers and rocks. I've seen all of those . . . anything else? I was hoping for something new," Snap said, betraying his disappointment.

"Well, there's the Greatest Show in the Forest," Harlena Gwin Falcon said hopefully.

"What show?" Snap said, perplexed, gazing into the falcon's left eye.

"Show?" Harlena Gwin Falcon drawled, considering how to explain. "It's like, when a flock of falcons, like me, for instance, huddle together and sing, 'kack-kack, kack-kack . . . kack-kack, kack-kack,' and do a claw shuffle like this," she said, hopping up and down on the branch and kicking one leg into the air and then the other. "Don't wolves do shows?"

"Oh, I get it . . . " Snap said, catching on. "It's when a pack of us sends up a chorus of howls, like this? Wuff, wuff, wuff . . . whoooo. Is that it?"

"Well sorta," Harlena Gwin Falcon said tentatively.

"Yeah, sure . . . that'd impress them," Snap said dejectedly. "No, I've gotta keep looking for wolves."

"You don't know what you're missing," Harlena Gwin Falcon said, then added, "I can tell you, you won't find anything that looks like you between here and big water . . . west." And looking south, she added, "That way? I'm not sure."

"Well, I can't go home," Snap said, rejecting the notion of retracing his steps.

Snap, eager to escape the bird's blabber, kept moving.

Harlena Gwin Falcon hovered over the retreating wolf, "I hope you find your wolves," she shouted, "But I wouldn't count on it." With those words of discouragement, she took to the air once more and winged her way west.

~~~

Snap was glad for the silence. He sat for a moment.

A gauzy, gray darkness settled over the rock cave where Snap found shelter. The tired wolf halfheartedly called into the frigid air and got no response. He curled his big legs close to his body, lay his big head on a pile of needles, and found sleep.
~~~

~ 20 ~

Into California

The next morning Snap awoke to bright sunshine. He felt rested and invigorated. He sniffed the crisp morning air again hoping to catch the scent of other wolves.

'It's a healthy place to live,' Snap said to himself. 'Gotta be wolves here somewhere.'

He sat on his haunches, looking across an ice-covered lake at a gaggle of Canada geese.

'Geese stay together,' he thought. 'Something tells them when and where to go . . . Why can't I hear that voice?'

A goose flapped gracefully into the air and settled on the lake's bank a hundred yards from the others.

Snap turned his head south, scanned a grove of alder lining the south shore of *Copco Lake,* and continued hiking south further into California.

Days later, Snap made friends with a couple of bears. He wondered how they could travel together without fighting over fish or berries, but he didn't ask.

He turned and trotted off to explore the foothills of *Mount Shasta.*

A curious outlaw-masked raccoon followed him for several miles, being careful not to get too close. At *Pigeon Hill,* Snap stopped for an extended rest.

"Why are you following me?" he called to the illusive raccoon that had settled on a rock a good distance away.

"I figured . . . somewhere along the way, you'd be downing a deer or something good to eat," the raccoon explained. "I like leftovers."

"You raccoons wear masks . . . why?" Snap asked, ignoring the raccoon's reference to food.

"Keeps the glare out of our eyes . . . We can see better day and night."

"I get it . . . " Snap said, inching toward the masked animal, "So, you ever see a wolf . . . day or night?"

"Wolf? You look like an overgrown coyote to me."

"Coyote!" Snap barked with disgust. "Nope, a wolf! What's your name?"

"Ron Raccoon."

"I'm Snap Wolf . . . intending to be Snap Alpha Wolf."

"Whatever that is," Ron said, mystified.

"Well, Ron, I'm here for a few days . . . hoping for better weather . . . I'll probably take a deer or an elk before I head south again. You can tag along if you can keep up . . . no skin off my shin."

~~~

The next weeks Snap and Ron relentlessly explored the hills and valleys south of Shasta for wolves.

Ron struggled to keep up.

"Since I left the Wallowas, I've spent months searching . . . " Snap said, trotting along. "I've sniffed the air, smelled every flower and weed along the way, hoping to detect tell-tail markings of a wolf . . . or wolves.

"I've called into nights . . . waited for responses. Inspected every living thing . . . the earth knows I've tried to find wolves. The heavens have witnessed my searching.

I'm going to make my way back to the Wallowas where I know there are wolves . . . even if I have to grovel."

"Too much for me," Ron said uneasily, shifting his weight. "Count me out . . . I'm staying here."

"Well, good fortune finding what makes you happy," Snap said. He chuckled and added, "Don't rob anybody."

"Huh?"

"Never mind . . . keep an eye out," Snap said warmly. Then, he turned tail and trotted off heading north back toward Oregon.
~~~

~ 21 ~

Giving up

By the time Snap crossed under the shadows of *Hatchet Mountain* heading north, the other side of winter had come and gone. Signs of spring were giving way to the rising heat of summer.

He was on his way home. He knew he would suffer derision from his wolf pack . . . but he would live through it. He would have to be content with being a subordinate . . . If he didn't submit, he would be an outcast . . . a lone wolf forever.

If he got lost, so what? In a way he'd been lost ever since he left Imnaha. Continuing to be lost was of no consequence.

He knew he could survive. He could certainly find enough food to sustain himself until he reached home . . . or wherever his wanderings took him.

Silverpuffs were blooming in prolific numbers on the northern slopes of *Mount Dorne* where Snap chose to spend a night. As the moon rose, Snap lifted his husky voice at the big saucer and called out. But, as had been the case every other night on his long journey, there was no answer.

The next morning he woke with a start. Before him not a tail's length away stood a giant eagle . . . head cocked with one eye focused on him. It was Rusty.

"Rusty! You startled me," Snap complained. "What's the matter with you . . . you know how I . . . we wolves can be when we are startled . . . Lucky I didn't attack you."

"I was watching your whiskers . . . " Rusty chuckled, "They give you away . . . Haven't seen you in an owl's age. Where you been?"

"Went south . . . you know . . . looking . . . "

"Yeah, I know . . . looking for wolves . . . no luck, huh?"

"Everything else but wolves. I decided to go back to the Imnaha Valley . . . back home."

"Saw your mom a couple of moons ago . . . she asked about you."

"She did?" Snap asked excitedly.

"Yeah, you know the nature of wolf-moms."

"Wow," Snap said.

"She asked about you, but I wouldn't get too excited. She has another litter of pups to care for. Not sure she needs to see you all that much."

"Oh," Snap said, unable to hide his disappointment.

"Makes sense, Snap," Rusty explained, "She is proud of you . . . certain you would find your own pack and become an alpha."

"Yeah, and I'm not," Snap said dejectedly, looking at dark clouds gathering in the west, " . . . she'd be ashamed of me."

"No! Your mom's moved on . . . that's all, and so should you," Rusty counseled.

"I'm ashamed," Snap said almost to himself.

"Listen! You've got nothing to be ashamed of. It's not your fault that there are no wolves here . . . well, none almost anywhere anymore. You've got to move on . . . you can be an alpha for yourself . . . and me . . . you are my alpha," Rusty said.

"You think? Nah . . . what can I do for you?"

"Be the best wolf you can be . . . that's all that's required of you . . . be the best wolf you can be and you'll be . . . Snap Alpha Wolf," Rusty said, emphasizing Snap's name.

"The lone wanderer is what I'll continue to be," Snap

said dejectedly, thinking about the hundreds of miles he'd traveled alone trying to find a mate.

"You don't have to be alone. You need family. That's what you need."

"Sure, gophers, rats and porcupine . . . some family," Snap returned.

"Gophers, rats and porcupine can be family . . . " the big bird paused. A sudden idea hit him. "Listen," he continued excitedly, "you should head for *Coggins Saddle*," Rusty paused again, lifting one of his big claws to do some calculating.

"Why?"

"I'm telling you . . . It's only a day or two west of here for a quick paced traveler like you."

"So . . . what's at Coggins Saddle?"

"What's at Coggins Saddle?" Rusty shouted, "Why . . . the Greatest Show in the Forest, That's what's at Coggins Saddle."

"And?"

"And summer's here . . . It will take place in a couple of days. Rehearsals are in progress as we speak . . . You get over there . . . Toby Pig will be thrilled to have a wolf be a part of the Spectacle." Rusty paused, laughing excitedly at his breakthrough idea. "No one in the *Siskiyou's* knows what a wolf looks like . . . you'll be the blockbuster attraction."

"Remember the woodpecker pecking contest up north?" Rusty prodded.

"Yeah," Snap said, fondly recalling the event.

"It's something like that . . . only more spectacular. The Rogue River Eagle Federation is sending a delegation of eagles to do diving exhibitions at the end of the parade. I'll be leading them."

"Too much for me . . . " Snap said listlessly and dejectedly added, "What you are saying is more than I can handle . . . I think I'll just head north . . . spend the summer at Crater Lake . . . then on to . . . "

"I won't let you do it!" Rusty interrupted. " . . . All alone while hundreds of animals are celebrating at Coggins . . . I won't let you do it."

"You may be Rusty Eagle . . . the biggest of the birds, but you can't boss a wolf."

"I'm not bossing," Rusty protested, "just trying to persuade you to join the Greatest Show in the Forest . . . that's all . . . make lots of friends. You'll like it."

"Sounds bossy to me," Snap snapped.

"Sorry, I didn't mean to . . . Listen, it's not far out of your way . . . getting to Crater Lake . . . It won't hurt you to stop by and see . . . will it?'

Snap lumbered around Rusty. "I guess I can do that," he finally said to the big bird.

"Good, I'll fly ahead. Maybe . . . I'll tell them you are

coming," Rusty said, taking flight. "You promised . . . see you tomorrow."

"Maybe the day after . . . " Snap shouted to the soaring eagle. He watched Rusty disappear behind the tall fir trees west of *Grizzly Butte.*

Snap gazed around . . . looking in the direction he had come and to the north. Then, he began trotting west into another unknown . . . toward Coggins Saddle and yet another new adventure.

~ 22 ~

The answer

Snap found himself trotting along a fir needle covered deer trail . . . He had told Rusty he would see him at Coggins Saddle . . . see the big eagle at The Greatest . . . something or other . . . in the Forest.

It would be an easy thing to go there . . . for a wolf . . . to hike through open forests, over hills, along streams and rivers. Yes, easy, but his heart wasn't in it.

He hadn't come to the end of the world like he feared he might . . . but he'd become increasingly convinced that, even if he had found where the world ends, he would not have found another wolf.

No . . . not the end of the world, but the end of his search.

Celebrate? What was there for him to celebrate? A lone wolf among pairs . . . while crowds of other animals frolicked each with its own kind . . . enjoying each other's company . . . what was there in that for him to celebrate?

No, he would change course again . . . head north and east back toward Imnaha, toward home . . . toward momma and the fate of a servile wolf.

"Rusty will understand," he said out loud, pausing at a fork in the trail . . . He sniffed the air, trotted off north and into the woods and heading in the opposite direction from Coggins Saddle.

As he traveled, he found increasing evidence that bigs were everywhere. He'd made a point of avoiding their groups of dwellings they called "towns" and "cities."

He settled for the night in a lush meadow near a creek. A cool wind ripped at the branches of the trees through which Snap could see the glow of light rising from where the bigs were living. He'd seen those balls of light many times at night, since leaving the Wallowas.

He'd wondered why bigs lit their nights. "Do they have to? Are they afraid? Wolves can see well at night. Apparently, bigs can't."

Without bothering to raise his accustomed call into

the night, Snap curled into a ball in a pile of pine needles and waited for sleep . . . He was on the verge of a disturbing dream.

The crash of a falling tree branch nearby snapped him into consciousness. The phantom nightmare had lasted only a few moments.

For a while he lay listening to the whistling wind. Distant voices mingled with nature's songs, urging Snap to be strong and courageous.

"If I were a real alpha, I'd call into the night . . . I'd have to," he said to the darkness. He arose from his pine needle bed, took a few steps to a large boulder half buried in the ground.

A full moon hung bright above the tree line to the east. Snap raised his nose into the air, laid his ears back, opened his jaws wide and emitted a long mournful howl.

His ears shot up. He thought he heard an answer . . . it sounded like a wolf . . . but he couldn't be sure. 'Probably a coyote,' he thought. Nevertheless, he scooted back onto the rock and repeated his wolf cry. A faint answer sounded.

'Could it be . . . could it be a wolf?' he allowed himself to think.

He called again . . . and again an answer came . . . 'It is a wolf,' he thought. 'But . . . No! . . . maybe not. Did he want the voice to be a wolf so badly he let his imagination morph coyote sounds into a wolf's call?'

Other than the sound of his own voice, he'd not heard an authentic wolf cry for months. He had to be sure. He called again . . . this time he reached into his lungs for the tones and force of an alpha wolf.

The answer came again . . . this time it seemed closer. His heart raced.

He had to get closer . . . His nose sucked in a lung full of air in hopes of catching the scent. The air was loaded with smells of many other animals but not a wolf. He concluded that he was upwind of it.

Never mind . . . He jumped from the rock and dashed off through the dark understory in the direction of the voice. The bright moon highlighted the terrain.

Thick foliage slowed his progress . . . heavy branches beat his face, chest, and legs. Despite the resistance he surged forward.

Suddenly, Snap broke into a clearing beneath a canopy of hemlock, fir, and vine maple. He stopped . . . surprised and pleased at what he saw.

Crouched before him at the ready and cautiously eyeing him was an adult female wolf.

For a long moment Snap stared at the appealing sight. Even in the ambient light he could see that the lady wolf was different from the wolves of the Imnaha pack. She was black.

"Who are you? Where're you from?" she asked with a guarded growl . . . "Keep your distance!"

It seemed clear to him that she wasn't afraid of him . . . just cautious. "I'm Snap . . . from Imnaha."

"Where's that?"

"Yeah, where?" Snap chuckled. "So far . . . so far you can't imagine . . . many and many sunsets and many more . . . so far I thought I'd never see another wolf again . . . I'm glad to find that I was wrong . . . you alone?"

"I may be . . . trying to decide," she answered, "My pack's over the mountains . . . hidden from everything."

"Like me," Snap said warmly.

"I got tired of being hidden from everything . . . so I left . . . came here . . . scary being alone."

"And lonely," Snap added. "What's your name . . . can I know?"

"I'm Ebony, Snap. Glad you yelled at the moon. I was beginning to think that I would have to go back home . . . back to hiding."

"Seems right to me . . . that we hang out together . . . do you think?"

"Hanging out . . . hanging out . . . seems right to me too . . . can't see you all that well in the dark . . . but you look alpha enough."

Snap was stunned . . . 'Alpha enough,' she'd said. All that time and all those hundreds of miles from Imnaha, dreaming of becoming an alpha male wolf and Ebony seemed to have recognized it. She had said it . . . that almost made it true.

Now all he needed was to find out if Ebony wanted more than just hanging out . . . does she want to be family . . . together. He wanted to ask her but . . . no . . . he'd wait until they got to know each other better and to give him time to find the courage.

"I'll bet you are even prettier in the daylight than you are in the moonlight," he finally said.

Ebony merely looked at Snap and grinned.

"If you want to . . . " Snap eagerly proceeded, "there's an animal celebration coming up not far from here . . . over in Coggins Saddle," he paused, reading the perplexed look in Ebony's eyes. "Rusty Eagle told me that . . . told me that . . . well, Rusty Eagle knows everything and he says all the animals living in this part of the forest are doing a parade . . . not far from here . . . ."

"Snap," Ebony interrupted calmly, "I don't know Rusty Eagle or where Coggins Saddle is or what a parade is? But, if you're wondering if I will go with you . . . the answer is, yes!"

Snap couldn't help it. He leaped high over a clump of sword fern. When he came down, he raised his nose high into the air and called as if his joy could reach all the way to Imnaha.

"I'm tired," Ebony said. "Know where we can bed down?"

"By this rock . . . we can rest here," Snap said, leading Ebony to his pine needle pad.

Ebony turned around twice in a tight circle, then, settled into a curled up ball and almost immediately fell asleep.

Snap lay beside her trying to resurrect the nightmare he'd had earlier about being a subordinate wolf forever. He could only remember snatches of it. But he fell asleep content that, if the dream came again, he was pretty sure he knew how it would end.

~ 23 ~

The Greatest Show in the Forest

Rusty Eagle, who had been watching the excitement from the air, settled on a boulder and began advising a band of coyotes. "There is a pattern . . . well, can be a pattern," he said. "All you need is a common thread holding your movements together in a pleasing pattern."

"Hey Rusty!" Tag and Alex said at the same time. The two coyotes looked at one another, surprised that the other was a friend of the famous eagle.

Tag deferred to Alex.

"Yeah? Well, you going to be the thread?" Alex asked the big eagle.

Rusty laughed as only an eagle can laugh, "Not me . . . me flapping near the ground would kick up enough dust . . . obscure everything . . . No . . . look, the thread you need is coming this way," Rusty concluded, focusing his eagle eyes on two approaching figures.

It was Snap and Ebony.

Alex's eyes popped. He had never seen anything like the animals trotting into the clearing. The Siskiyou coyotes' muscles tensed, ready to run, if necessary . . . but Tag, Becky, and Lillie's calmness told them that they weren't afraid.

"Hey, Snap!" Tag called. "Is it really you?"

"What's left of me after wandering around those mountains forever," Snap laughed.

"Hi Snap," Lillie said sweetly, "Glad to see you again. Who's your lady friend?"

"Hi Lillie . . . Hi Becky," Snap responded brightly. "This is Ebony!"

They just stood there dumbfounded.

Snap continued, " . . . met her yesterday . . . last night."

"Found what you were looking for . . . did you?" Tag smiled.

"Sure have," Snap said boldly and added. "She's from

Hidden Mountain a long way east," he gestured, tossing his head.

"Well, we're glad you're here," Tag said. "We could use your help."

Snap was surprised. He couldn't imagine what trouble could have befallen a band of coyotes. "What's the trouble?"

"No trouble really, but we're supposed to be in The Greatest Show in the Forest . . . and . . . we've got a routine going but Toby doesn't like it. Rusty says it needs a thread . . . "

"Yeah, the coyote leap-over could be an outstanding piece," Rusty said, "If it had something to hold it together . . . a powerful rhythmic thread as it were."

"Greatest Show in the Forest. Yeah, Rusty told me about it," Snap said. "I understand it's kinda like the woodpecker pecking contest."

"Kinda," Rusty said, only different . . . all the animals living in *Siskiyou Forest* are in it . . . It's a great celebration."

"Count us in. What do we do?" Snap asked.

"Snap and Ebony will make the missing thread for your coyote leap-over routine," Rusty said. "Why don't you give it a try?"

"Here's the way it works," Rusty suggested, "Snap and Ebony lead the procession trotting side by side in a straight line. You others . . . you five coyotes . . . in turn jump over both of them in a crisscross pattern, making your movements look like a band of coyotes . . . Give it a try. Meanwhile, I'm off to tweak the eagle-dive. See you later." Rusty was gone.

For the next long while the five coyotes and their new friends worked on Rusty's coyote/wolf act. Two hours later they had woven the routine into a flawless showpiece.

When Toby Pig showed up in the late afternoon, he was astonished. A concert of coyotes had created a bounding, rhythmic, braided dance led by two large, graceful wolves . . . bigger and powerful in ways he'd never seen before.

~ 24 ~

An alpha wolf at last

Later that day, Snap and Ebony led the parade and it was even better than anyone could have imagined. After it was over, of course, there was a lot of curiosity among the Siskiyou animal community over the presence of the pair of wolves who had come among them. The wild excitement lasted into the evening. Then, it subsided into quiet conversation . . . to soft murmurs, and finally into distant sounds of slumber.

But for Snap it was different. Finding Ebony had brought the bewildering world into focus for him. He looked at Ebony's sleek, shiny coat. She was beautiful . . . The most beautiful wolf he'd ever seen. For a long while he sat gazing at Ebony sleeping peacefully before him. Tomorrow and every day after would be a new adventure for him.

Finally, he carefully crawled out of the cave and into the damp air. He climbed onto a pile of rocks next to the cave entrance.

He howled into the night. But this time his tone was different . . . His elongated "woof, woof . . . Woooooooooo" no longer had the tone of a lonely wolf.

He sat on his haunches for a long while thinking about Imnaha. He thought about how far he'd come. He was sure the Imnaha pack would be astonished at all that had happened to him. But he felt sure that his father would approve of him settling in the *Siskiyou Mountains,* even among coyotes and other strangers.

He called again into the night. He listened for a wolf response . . . Of course, none came . . . only the disturbed murmurs of those slumbering nearby and the distant howl of coyotes celebrating life.

But it no longer mattered. Snap looked at the silver moon rising above the tree line to the east.

"Mom would like what my journey has done to me," he said to the shining disk hanging in the night sky. "Maybe you can tell her that I am doing good . . . Tell her I'm okay." He paused, studying the glowing image. A wisp of a cloud passed over the moon. "Tell her I like where I am . . . I like who I am."

He crawled into the cave and laid down next to Ebony, knowing that his mother would like the charming wolf he'd found, and that she would be proud of Snap, her courageous Alpha Wolf son.

Vocabulary

Abrasive — something capable of polishing a hard surface by rubbing or grinding

Alpha — the dominant animal or human in a particular group

Alpine — relating to high mountains

Ambient — relating to immediate surroundings of something

Ammunition — a supply or quantity of bullets

Apex — the top or highest part of something

Appealing — attractive or interesting

Apropos — with reference to or concerning

Authentic — real

Basalt — a dark, fine-grained volcanic rock

Big saucer — in this story it means the moon

Bravado — to show boldness to impress or intimidate someone

Butte — an isolated hill with steep sides and a float top (but narrower than a mesa)

Calculating — act in a scheming and ruthless way

Canopy — uppermost trees or branches of the trees in a forest

Carrion — the decaying flesh of a dead animal

Clarified — make less confused

Commiserated — expressed or felt sympathy or pity for

Compelled — forced to do something

Conceded — admitting something is true after first denying it

Crooned — hum or sing in a soft low voice

Crouched — sit is a position where the knees are bent

Dejectedly — sad or depressed

Derision — ridicule or mockery

Elongated — unusually longer than it is wide

Emphasizing — give special importance to

Exhibition — a public display of items of interest

Feint — a deceptive movement or pretended blow or thrust

Fisher — a large brown martin valued for its fur

Fork in the trail — a place where the road divides

Frolicked — cheerful, merry or playful

Gnawing — worrying or distressing

Grovel — lie on the ground face down

Haunches — a buttock and thigh considered together in an animal or a human

Hostile — unfriendly

Hovered — remain in one place in the air

Hurtling — move or cause to move at great speed

Illusive — deceptive — can't get a hold of

Impasse — a situation in which no progress is possible

Intimidating — frighten or overawe someone to make them do what you want

Invigorated — give strength to

Listlessly — lacking energy or enthusiasm

Lumbered — move in a slow, heavy, awkward way

Mark — a target

Marrow — a soft fatty substance in the cavities of bones

Mincing — dainty in manner or gait

Mocking — making fun of someone or something in a cruel way

Morph — change smoothly in small gradual steps

Mulling — thinking about

Negotiate — Try to reach an agreement

Nostalgia — a sentimental longing for the past

Obscure — not important or well known

Outcast — not accepted by the rest

Paralleling — Side by side

Permeated — spread throughout something

Perplexed — completely baffled or confused

Persistent — continuing firmly in a course of action

Phantom — a ghost

Pika — a small mammal with rounded ears, short limbs and small tail

Pipe Dream — an unattainable or fanciful hope or scheme

Pivoted — the central point on which something turns

Plateau — An area of relatively level high ground

Plight — a dangerous, difficult or otherwise unfortunate situation

Predators — an animal that preys on others

Prickly pear — a cactus with jointed stems and flattened sections

Prolific — large numbers or quantities

Protective system — in a skunk it is spraying an awful smell

Reassured —having removed all doubt

Rejecting — dismiss as not complete or not good enough

Relentless — constant

Servile — willing to serve or please others

Servitude — being a slave

Shin — the front of the leg below the knee

Spectacle — a striking performance or display

Splendor — magnificent and splendid appearance

Straggling — move slowly some distance behind the those in front

Subordinate — lowers in rank or position — less important

Subservient — be prepared to obey others without question

Tenacious — tending to keep a firm hold of something

Tentatively — not certain or fixed

Treacherous — guilty of involving betrayal or deception

Underbrush — shrubs and small trees in a forest

Understory — a layer of vegetation beneath the trees in the forest

Undulating — having a wavy form or outline

Urge — a strong desire or impulse

Vacillated — waver between different opinions or actions

Verge — an edge or border

Vultures — a large bird of prey that feeds chiefly on carrion (decaying animals)

Zigzagging — a line or course making right and left turns

Oregon place names

Bear Creek
Beeler Ridge
Blue Mountains
Cascade Mountains
Cayuse Meadow
Central Oregon
Coggins Saddle
Columbia River
Copco Lake
Crater Lake
Dooley Mountain
Goose Creek
Granite Mountain
Grizzly Butte
Hatchet Mountain
Hells Canyon
Hidden Mountain
Hole-in-the-Ground
Horse Creek
Imnaha River
Imnaha Valley

Jump-off-Joe Mountain
Little Eagle Creek
Malheur River
Mount Dorne
Mount Shasta
Paulina Peak
Pigeon Hill
Pine Lake
Powder River
Red Mountain
Salmon River
Scott Mountain
Seven Devils
Sheep Mountain
Siskiyou Forest
Siskiyou Mountains
Snake River
Umpqua National Forest
Wallowa County
Wallowa Mountains
Willow Lake
Wolf Creek
Wolf Mountain
Zumwalt Prairie

Morris R. Pike, author

Born in Texas and raised in Oregon, Dr. Pike earned his undergraduate degree at Cascade College, his Masters in Education at the University of Oregon and a PhD in Theatre at Kent State University.

He taught both grade school and high school in Cottage Grove, Oregon, college at Cascade College in Portland, Oregon and Malone College in Canton, Ohio and retired in 1998 as Professor Emeritus from Vanguard University in Costa Mesa, California.

In his retirement he conceived the irascible and loveable pirate Captain Book, who appears at libraries, classrooms and hospitals inspiring children to read. To date he has given away more than 100,000 free books to children who would not otherwise have them.

A recipient of many service awards and honors, Dr. Pike's hobbies include photography, woodworking, gardening, jewelry making and writing fiction. He has written, produced and directed a number of sketches and musicals during his teaching career including "The Eighth from Adam" and an allegory about Noah called "You Are a First Class Nut." He has written three novels and several children's stories for his grandchildren (see Stories for Children and Up at countrytraveleronline.com).

Dr. Pike currently lives in Encinitas, California.

Chris Sheets, illustrator

Inheriting a bent for acting from his mother and a talent for art from his father, Chris Sheets is successful at both. Born and raised in Los Angeles, Chris earned a Bachelor in Communication (with an emphasis in theater) at Southern California College, Costa Mesa, California (now Vanguard University), and a Masters of Arts from Western Washington University in Bellingham, Washington.

In addition to a variety of acting jobs, he performs improvisational theater, comedy sketches and puppetry at Jim Henson Company Studios.

To illustrate *A Diary of Snap Wolf's Journey to Find a Mate,* Chris read only one chapter at a time before picking and completing each illustration. Once he determined the image he wanted, he penned line drawings on the brown paper pages of a book he bought years ago in Hong Kong. He adds the background and watercolor last.

Chris can be reached at chris.sheets@gmail.com